Approaching Equilibrium

Short stories by David MacNeill

Approaching Equilibrium

Short stories by David MacNeill
Edited by Leslie Judd MacNeill
Cover illustration by Polly Powell

Copyright David MacNeill ©2022 All Rights Reserved
All Contents Registered DETAIB (IP-SENSE 0.92)

Copyright 2022 Byrnum Downs House LLC

ISBN 9798849210933

OTHER TITLES BY DAVID MACNEILL AVAILABLE SOON FROM BYRNUM DOWNS HOUSE:

No Crying In Space

One Night On Ganymede

Another Day, Another Rocket

I Know What Happens Tomorrow

The Helmet-cam Diaries

Zero G Wiz

Just Passing Through The Wormhole

The Adventures of Captain Wavebender

Stupid Bloody Robot

A Visitor's Guide to Proxima Centauri

Space Is A Bitch And Then You Die

Down And Out on Luna

Starcharts for Dummies

Prologue

It was three in the morning on a warm midsummer night, sitting on the patio, facing southwest. From this latitude, Luna and the planets and the unreachable stars always look more interesting in that orientation — one can more easily perceive their slow movements.

I thought about a close friend who left this rock far too soon. What would I say to him if I could go back, if only for a few minutes, that would prevent his untimely passing? What would that mean to all those who knew and loved him?

The story came quickly, like it wanted to be told. The next night, it picked up where it had left off, as the good ones always do. I know from a lifetime of songwriting that these things must be dutifully captured else bad things happen. It is perhaps my only superstition and it has served me well.

Thus my first story was born. I thought it was a one-off, a mere phantasm, a talking dream, but others soon followed in its wake. The undiscovered country now intruded on the one I know all too well.

I am mostly interested in the consequences of decisions we make today on our future. Nothing would please me more than to elicit such musings in you as you read these stories, spanning from the day after tomorrow to the last syllable of recorded time. ~DM

Table of Contents

The Promise Of No Regrets	7
Time Machine	18
MurderChef	21
At Least I Have a Heart	27
The Peace Weapon	34
Hot for 'Naut	49
NeuroType	58
Re: The Solitaire™	63
The Value Of Nothing	65
Big Dog	78
Approaching Equilibrium	83

The Promise Of No Regrets

"You have 17 minutes 27 seconds before you return. You will arrive precisely where you departed from. When you contact your friend, he will not believe that you are who you claim to be, so stick to your script.

"Keep in mind that whatever timeline changes you cause will occur in a different verse created by your friend's actions, but nothing will change in ours. It is impossible to observe or enter another verse—it's a brick wall of physics. You can only hope your friend's world will be better because you were there, but you can never know if you made any difference."

"I'm good to go, chief."

"One more thing: Everyone has doubts at this point in their journey; I sure as hell did when I went on mine. But I got to see my dad, healthy and lucid, fully capable of understanding my words. It was transformative for me, knowing he lived on for many years in another verse, understanding who I was and what he meant to me and my mother.

"You go back to help them, then return having helped yourself just as much. Don't forget it."

The yellow eCab dropped Marc off at East Portal Park. In the distance to the west, he saw his friend Eric's memorial bench with the bronze plaque that his family commissioned, overlooking the area where they threw frisbees and played guitars and drank beer.

He walked to the spot on the rise by the baseball diamond and waited for the designated moment. *I may see myself at 22!* he thought. He walked to the trees a short distance away, out of line of sight where Eric had asked to meet. Suddenly appearing is considered bad form—it scares the shit out of people and complicates things. Anyone living prior to December 2029 will not have any idea how jumps work. Everyone has seen the videos; it's only funny the first time.

"Have a safe jump, and good luck!" texted the chief.

The trainers weren't kidding: it happens instantaneously. He felt like he had just bumped into something in the dark that wasn't supposed to be there.

All the trees were smaller, the sky bluer, and old Italian men milled around what was then a bocci ball court.

"Hello Eric. Young Marc will be here soon. I am old Marc, 72 to be exact. I have traveled here to deliver a message. I know what you are going to ask me today: You want my blessing to date Dawn. Hear me out. I don't have much time."

Eric looked at him as though he was insane, but continued to listen with a smirk. *Have I really changed so much that he can't see it's me?* Marc said to himself. *How depressing is that?*

"If I say yes, you will marry Dawn in about two years. She doesn't really want children, but you talk her into it. You will buy a pleasant duplex in West Sacramento. You will work as an instructor at a small culinary institute and she will continue working at UPS.

Things go fairly smoothly, but after ten years or so, you eventually separate over your heavy drinking and because she suspects you of having an affair with one of your students. She throws you out of the house. You had a hydrocodone prescription for your back pain and faxed copies to pharmacies in Canada and Mexico. In your isolation, you become addicted to opioids and drink even more than before.

"One morning, on your way to pick up one of your kids to drive her to Country Day School in Fair Oaks, you lose control and crash your small truck into a tree on the levee road from your little rented house in Clarksburg, narrowly escaping driving into the river. There are pills all over the cab when they haul you out, your abdomen crushed by the steering wheel. After a slow decline, you die in your mother's arms eleven months later from your injuries. You are 51 years old. Dr. James told me at your wake that you died the moment you hit that tree.

"So if I answer no to your question, your untimely death is preventable, but at a steep cost. There is an unavoidable trade-off if you do not pursue Dawn. Today is the pivotal moment that can let you either continue on your tragic timeline, or choose another one for yourself—and for her."

Eric said, "So...say I believed this madness, now that I know all this I can avoid the accident, right? Is that what you're saying?"

"Sorry, but no. Even with this new knowledge, you cannot change your fate in my timeline, only in yours. For me, it is history. Your two children will live on in my timeline, but they will not be born in yours if you walk away from her today. That is, obviously, the bad part. The good part is that you probably get to live three or four decades longer.

"Consider this too: Stay here and you will never reach your potential, never write that novel you nurture in your head. And neither will Dawn. She yearns to be an artist, but that will prove impossible what with raising the kids and working nights. And consider the unspeakably tragic impact your death brings to your family and friends, especially your mother—she was never the same after, man."

Eric said, "This is a joke, right? Not very funny."

"I wish it was, but no. It's real. Only you can make this call."

Marc looked at his first-gen steel Apple Watch, a technology that will not be invented for decades . Just a few minutes left…

"I have to be going soon. One more thing you need to know. It's not all unicorns and rainbows in the 21st century. It's pretty bad, man, and it's still getting worse in my time. But even such a fucked up world would be better with you in it, and that's why I am using my shot to change the past to tell you this. I assure you, there is no shortage of things I would *love* to change about my life, but this is the one that hurt us all the most, that feels the most unfair."

After another glance at his watch, Marc saw young Marc enter the park from the east in the distance. He remembers that leather jacket and wished he had kept it instead of giving it to that girl. He wished there was time to tell that young man to keep it forever but…

"It's time. It was great to see you again, my friend."

Marc walked briskly away. With only seconds left before the return jump, he approached the trees near the bocci court and...

⌘

Modern day. The sky was pale orange, the air smelled like smoke, and the trees were tall again. The old bocci men and their charming court had been replaced by boisterous hipsters playing shuffleboard. Strangely, the return jump didn't disorient him at all. It was more like a quick cut in a movie of the same scene from day to dusk.

"How did it go? How do you feel? Ready to talk?" texted the chief.

"Feel ok. I think it went well. He might have seen me jump, but compared to what I had just told him, I doubt he would be surprised. I'll wait for you at the memorial bench on the northwest corner of the park."

The chief, seated in a white van a quarter mile away, scanned the park's security camera feed on his laptop.

"Uh Marc, there *is* no bench on the park's northwest corner."

"Check again. I saw it just before the first jump."

He walked toward the bench. It was gone with no sign that it ever existed.

Stunned, Marc realized that if the bench isn't there then Eric never died, but that can't be true here.

He looked at the contacts in his phone and saw Eric's name was there along with a spouse named Sally, followed by the names of three children. He scrolled to his own card and saw a Sacramento phone number and an address a few blocks away, followed by nothing.

"Something's wrong. This is wrong. Where is Layla? Where's Enid? They're just...gone? I don't recognize most of these other names either. We don't live in the big blue house in Walnut Creek anymore? Did I break something? Have I crossed into the verse Eric's decision caused?"

The chief said, after a pause, "Marc, you have always lived in East Sacramento and you know what you are suggesting is impossible. We need to get you to the doc now. I'm on my way..."

Marc dropped his arm to his side and processed for a long moment, numb. *This can't be happening*, he said in his head. The park swam beneath him and he felt sick. The chief was a distant voice in his hand. One terrible thought surfaced: *Did I change myself so much that I went with him?*

"Never mind, chief. I can find my way home."

⌘

"Layla? Layla Jack? It's Marc Olsen. You probably don't remember me, but you are a friend from my past. I just wanted to say hello and see how you are doing."

"Sorry, I don't remember you. Were we at UNR together?"

"We worked together at that little Apple shop in Rancho Cordova, after you left Businessland?"

"I did work there for a time, then went into teaching before I launched my consulting business. I'm really sorry but I have no memory of you."

"I didn't think you would. Just thought of you and wondered how you were."

"Um...well, I got married, had two children, and now I'm a happily retired grandmother."

"That's wonderful to hear. Well okay, I won't take up any more of your time. Thanks for taking my call, Layla."

"No problem...Marc, right?"

"That's what they tell me, yep."

"Well, good bye then."

"Farewell, Layla."

⌘

The docs told him his post-jump symptoms were an anomaly and that there was nothing they could do. Marc was sure they thought he was delusional. They recommended he proceed as though he had suffered massive memory loss and that the only prescription was to connect with people from his past that might fill in the lost details of his fifty-year memory hole.

He had been happily married for 35 years and they had a 33 year-old daughter. Now his wife doesn't remember ever knowing him and his daughter was never born. He was alone in a place that looked the same, but was utterly unfamiliar. *'I don't recall anything about this shit in the brochure,'* he thought, then laughed until he cried inconsolably.

Aside from his personal loss, the world at large was exactly as he had left it, but this was no surprise to him. As Bogart said, "...the problems of three little people don't amount to a hill of beans in this crazy world."

⌘

The chief's face on Marc's screen was a caricature of seriousness.

"Marc, I remind you that the NDAs you signed are valid in this verse and all the others", said the chief, breaking into a wry smile. "Privately, I want you to know that I believe you. There has been considerable internal discussion about you and we have a team outside our main group working on it."

"Have they come up with anything?"

"Well...yes. There are only two possible explanations. One hypothesis is that you jumped at the precise moment your friend changed his mind. In effect, you *did* jump into his new verse along with him. If that's what actually happened, that means your anomaly could possibly be controlled and replicated. Problem is, how do we find volunteers to test it? They would have to be willing to leave their verse, with totally unknown consequences, such as those you claim to have experienced."

"What about people who would give anything just to live in another verse, a better verse? There must be thousands..."

"We thought of that and are considering recruiting incarcerated individuals, particularly those on death row in the few states that have yet to outlaw capital punishment."

"That has a certain poetic justice to it, I guess. The rub is that the authorities would never know what happens to them, just as you know nothing of my life in the verse I left."

"Right. The cops can never know what they do in their new verse, and cops really hate losing touch with their, um, *clients*. The legal and political implications are staggering. Frankly, no one wants to touch this."

"Ok. What's the second explanation?"

The chief's face became pinched and a bit sad. "The second hypothesis is infinitely more problematic: You didn't jump to a new verse at all. Somehow, something you did changed *this* verse. If that turns out to be true, I'm probably out of a job. It takes our harmless tech and makes it radioactive. The black suits from DC would shut us down overnight and beat our plowshare into a sword, if you will. Time travel in this verse would be the most powerful weapon imaginable."

⌘

"Did I tell you that I met with Dawn last week, chief? She told me that we got back together for about six years. Then I got a job at Apple and had to relocate to Cupertino but she didn't want to move. Her gallery was just then breaking even. Perhaps I could have convinced her to move her whole operation. Could I jump back and do that? I'm all alone here."

"Extremely inadvisable. The board would never approve it. We have short-jump testers who have made multiple trips, but the results so far have been troubling. Testers tend to fixate on correcting just one more thing with just one more jump—it becomes an addiction—and it gets worse the further back you jump. Marc, you jumped *fifty fucking years!*"

"Yeah, I can relate. I've only jumped once and I think about jumping again all the time. I dream about it, then wake up to this brave new world every day."

"I truly wish I could do more for you, Marc. But my job is to make people happier by removing their greatest regret, then empty their bank accounts for our investors. Who knows? Your anomaly may turn out to be a great new product for us."

After the call ended, Marc ruminated. Both hypotheses lead to one reality: The jump was, for him, a one-way trip. Could he reframe this loss from a tragedy into an opportunity? That's what Layla would do. After all, he *had* saved his best friend's life…

⌘

"Hello Eric! Can you talk now?"

"Sure thing. I'm just reading and nibbling on a pretty decent Pinot. You'd like it. What's up?"

"Do you remember when we met in the park five decades ago to talk about Dawn?"

"Ah, yes I do. I think I may have been high…"

"You weren't high, dude. I have something to tell you about that day, but first, please fill me in on what's happened in your life—in *our* life—since that day. I had an accident that resulted in decades of memory loss."

A perfectly normal life ensued for them both, it seems: The small victories. The heartaches. The thousand natural shocks that flesh is heir to. The accusations and the vindications. Brief brushes with fame and fortune, and long, lean times of anonymity. There were amusing stories that made him smile, even though he was not, technically speaking, *there*.

And eventually he thought, this undiscovered country was not so different from the one he knew. And it became more real each passing day. So he will have to learn to live with it. But what dreams may come?

— • • • —

Time Machine

James came in at 3:00 every day, rain or shine. He waved to the bartender, said, "The usual, please," then sat at his regular barstool on the far left end of the bar. He doffed his trilby and set it on the bar. Nobody wore trilbys unironically anymore, but James did. Your bowlers, your Borsalinos, your obnoxious fedoras—all the skinny young fellas looked faintly ridiculous in them. James appreciated their efforts to look like they were cool, that they had been around and stayed for tea, but these fresh-faced lads were all poseurs. They knew nothing of history, nothing of life—those hats wore *them*.

Mid-afternoons, the publican would usually serve him his Tanqueray and tonic. James would invariably order a Reuben unless the French Dip was on the special board by the door.

James ran a tab and never tipped, but on Christmas he always handed out envelopes with the names of every bartender neatly printed on them, each containing a crisp hundred dollar bill, fresh from the bank. As a rule, one does not tip the publican.

After some time had passed, James would lower his head a bit and talk silently to himself for hours. He seemed happy, smiling often and even quietly laughed from time to time. When the tavern was crowded and noisy late in the week or on a holiday, he would put his trilby back on and pull the brim down a bit. When he left his barstool for the restroom, he placed his trilby on it so no one would think he was gone.

James never talked to anyone unless he had to. When addressed, he would slowly turn to his interlocutor and politely respond as required. Many times the yuppies and hipsters or whatever they called themselves these days would attempt a friendly, boozy chat with the old man, but he would just smile and let them wear themselves out. He had nothing to say to anyone here beyond hello and goodbye.

One day just after James had seated himself, two hooded punks pointed their guns at the publican and robbed the place. They wielded matte black Model 1911 semi-autos, probably purchased as war surplus from a gun show out at the fairgrounds. James had one in his desk drawer at home that he brought home from the war. He thought at the time: Why would these fools rob a tavern with an extremely loud and deadly gun that leaves brass evidence wherever it is used? Idiots.

On September 11, 2001, James went to the tavern early. He had seen the towers fall that morning on TV like everybody else and it made him feel like he had been punched in the gut twice. The tavern was near the airport but there were no planes in the sky that day. He missed the sound of freedom a powerful airplane makes; years of flying navigator on B-17s will do that to a man.

Next day, James did not come to the tavern. The young bartender mentioned it to the publican. He replied, "They found him yesterday in his apartment."

"Sad. Funny old geezer, eh?" said the bartender. "I'm gonna miss him. Great hat. I always wondered who he was talking to?"

"Her name was Elizabeth, his fiancée. When he returned from the Pacific in '45, she had disappeared and he never found her. In those days, you could just start a new life elsewhere, without a trace. Women would change their name and *poof*, gone. No bloody Google or any of that social crap back then. You could just move on."

"Whoa. That barstool is gonna be hella empty from now on, boss."

The publican stopped polishing the rocks glass in his hand. After a long pause, he said, "That's no barstool, son. It's a goddamned time machine."

— • • • —

A tip of the trilby to songwriter Gary Burr for inspiring this story.

MurderChef

(Drum roll into main theme)

"It's MurderChef! A meal that's to die for!

(Level six applause track)

"Tonight we feature four female chefs from the American South. And here they are!:

• Mandy Brozman from Metairie, Louisiana!

• LaVaugn Williams from Mobile, Alabama!

• Luna Ramirez from Austin, Texas!

• and Veena Heisenberg from Jupiter, Florida!

"And here's our host, Biff Watanabe!"

(Level 7 applause track)

"Thank you, thank you, everyone, and welcome to MurderChef. First time viewers, here's how it works: Four chefs compete to make eight randomly selected audience members taste their food, for better or worse! No contestant has ever died on the show, but some came pretty close! The winning chef is the one who makes the most people deathly ill the fastest."

(Level 4 audience gasp track)

"No worries, friends. We have our own ER, plus a body regen station and revival staff at all times, and every taster gets a full cerebackup before we tape.

(Brief cut to backup and regen capsules backstage, backed with Level 3 audience oh track)

"Let's meet our first chef. Hello Mandy! Welcome to MurderChef! What's on the menu for our tasters tonight?"

⌘

Biff was not happy with the rough edit, and when Biff wasn't happy, nobody was happy.

"What the bloody fuck were you all thinking?" he yelled at the producer, the editor, and a cowering PA. "Garbage in, garbage out, right? I can't work with these dreary cows. What does this bollocks network pay you for, eh?"

Producer Sandra Damon replied, "It's a hell of a lot easier to find men than to find women who will commit murder for us. And after our last season closer, I don't blame them."

"Bollocks!" barked Biff. "That bloke was an insane ex-con who went way over the line with his dish. That dead taster was revived by the following morning —great television, eh?"

"Best ratings and more likes than ever, granted. But it scared a lot of potentials off."

"What does it say on your biz card, eh? What does it bloody say? 'Producer', eh? So produce me some fucking chefs who will try to kill people!"

Biff stomped out of the edit booth and down the hall, slamming every door he passed.

⌘

MurderChef was a hard show to pitch, even after a decade of body regens in every stripmall urgent care and cerebackup kiosks in every bigbox and stop-and-rob. Basic home regens get cheaper every year. The worst a victim could expect was to lose all memories since their last backup and have to wait a day or two for body repairs, maybe ten days for a new body. Murder was just not such a big deal anymore—more of an inconvenience, really.

Sandra sat in her little office, processing what Biff had said in his latest tantrum. She had to admit that her casting was pretty timid for last week's show. Only two tasters hurled on camera—they used to *all* hurl on every show last season. The show is supposed to be about psychotic chefs who try to kill people with food, not just make them nauseous. It had to look like, *feel* like, someone in the kitchen was trying to punish tasters for something they'd done. If the tasters left the soundstage on a stretcher, they had done their job.

Then Sandra had an idea: get prison cooks on the show. Who else had more hate for their customers than a prison cook? And if they got chefs from rival gangs, they might even murder each other!

⌘

Sandra found that it was a piece of cake to get incarcerated volunteers. Who wouldn't trade being inside for a shot at fame? She interviewed 56 candidates from all over the country and narrowed them down to eight: four men and four women. She coached them about hitting their marks, when to look at the camera and when not to, and how to project their voice to the boom mics. She cleaned them up, dressed them like pro chefs, and when she was satisfied with their look and delivery, sent a PA to fetch Biff from his office to have a look.

"Right!" he said. "Four of you will be on the show at a time. We tape two week's shows all in one day, so make sure your tasters get sick fast. I want to see blood and piss and shit here, people. Are you ready to kill some randos? *Are you bloody ready to kill?*"

Satisfied that he might actually get what he wanted for a change, Biff lounged in his lair, hammered a couple of scotches, and napped on his leather couch.

⌘

Chrissy, Biff's favorite PA, woke him gently and said, "It's time for final rehearsal, sir."

After grousing a bit while ogling Chrissy, he checked himself in his 180º mirror as she touched up his hair. *Note: Find out who Chrissy is seeing and if he/she works here, fire them,* he tapped into his phone.

Biff was optimistic. These chefs were the kind of people audiences love to hate, and that meant viewer engagement. Their dishes were pedestrian, of course, but looked delicious in a truck-stop-I-haven't-eaten-in-twelve-hours-so-what's-the-special-today? kind of way.

They didn't rehearse tasters selection, so the whole, two-episode dress rehearsal took about three hours. He liked what he saw and told the crew after that he was optimistic for a change, briskly thanked them, and returned to his lair to mentally undress Chrissy a bit more as he doffed his stage tux and changed into street clothes. His limo was waiting out back.

⌘

"Thank you, thank you, thank you, beautiful people, and welcome to MurderChef. First time viewers, here's how it works: Four chefs compete to make eight randomly selected audience members taste their food, for better or worse! No contestant has permanently died on the show, but last season's final episode was a really close call, right? Am I *right?* You know who you are, you lovely little devils.

(Level 4 audience applause track)

"As always, the winning chef is the one who makes the most people deathly ill in the least time.

(Level 5 audience gasp track)

"Now now, no worries, my friends. We have our own body regen station and revival staff at all times, and every taster gets a full cerebackup before we tape.

(Brief cut to backup and regen capsules backstage, with a Level 3 audience oh track)

"So let's get to it people, or just kill me now!

"Let's meet our first chef. Hello Lucille! Welcome to MurderChef! What's have you cooked up for our tasters tonight?"

⌘

The taping went off without a hitch. All eight tasters puked almost immediately and three of them collapsed on the stage and were gurneyed to the ER backstage.

Biff was very pleased and Sandra was relieved. She thought her job was on the line after last week's taping, but this mayhem was exactly what Biff and the show's backers wanted.

⌘

In the back of his limo, Biff and Chrissy celebrated with champagne and caviar on the drive up the hill to his mansion. He was in an expansive mood, as was Chrissy, who apparently had figured out what her boss wanted from her.

As the limo turned into the big curve up Mulholland, Biff ordered his driver to stop. The driver complied, but not fast enough: Biff puked explosively, then, coughing violently and drooling bloody vomit, started screaming, "Hospital NOW!" The driver looked back at Chrissy, then drove slowly up the hill to Biff's mansion.

"Don't worry, baby. He'll be dead before we arrive."

Chrissy smiled at her boyfriend and poured herself another glass of champagne.

— • • • —

At Least I Have a Heart

"I'm getting married to Ariel!" enthused Daniel as the band stood outside their rehearsal room on a vape and beer break.

Dead silence.

"Um…Why?" blurted the songwriter, immediately regretting stating the obvious.

"Ariel's a really terrific girl. We get along great and the sex is fantastic! And I don't think I could do any better than to marry my best friend."

"Well oKAY then!" said the songwriter, twisting his face into a simulacrum of happiness—eye wrinkles and all.

⌘

Ariel left him five years later. She said she didn't love him anymore and just walked away. Abandoned their two little kids too, so overnight Daniel became a single dad with full custody. Well into his fifties at that point and running his own electronics repair business from his home, he had his hands more full than they had ever been in his lifelong bachelorhood. He stepped up admirably and did his best, read all the books and did everything right, but his friends could see it was taking its toll on his already imperfect health. Now Daniel could add a big fat broken heart to his other ailments.

⌘

"Was it a heart attack, doc?"

"Technically, no. Your artificial heart glitched for three seconds, long enough for you to collapse. We call it a techno-infarction. That unit should be replaced."

"I can't afford that! HeartUS guaranteed it to last 25 years before replacement and it's only been in there for three years! I had to beg for enough money to get it installed…"

"I am sorry to tell you that HeartUS was bought out by a Taiwanese competitor last year and shut down. They were required by law to contact you about it."

"I never received *anything* from them. So I'm screwed here, right?"

"I'm afraid so, Daniel."

⌘

At home the next day, Daniel went into full-tilt nerd research mode. He used the HeartUS app on his phone to run diags and found nothing out of the ordinary outside of the three second blip that sent him to the ER. Every test was nominal, as was every comparative performance stat uploaded by thousands of other recipients using the same device with the same firmware. He was just standing in his workshop looking at an oscilloscope and *boom* out go the lights. It didn't make any sense.

He couldn't do anything about it in his current situation, two little kids and a business that wasn't making ends meet. Plenty of work coming in but the competition from a new national chain that had opened last year had forced him to lower his hourly rate nearly in half. His bills had backed up for months and he didn't know what to do except work longer hours and spend even less time being a single dad.

⌘

"You are now over three months late on alimony. I gave you a warning shot. Are you listening now? I still own that heart of yours and I have full access to it from the app you installed on my phone. My dad paid for most of it, so it's mine. Nothing in the divorce settlement said anything about medical devices. Pay up, deadbeat!" texted Ariel at three in the morning.

Daniel could not believe anyone could be so cruel. Even though she had been granted regular visitation rights, her time with the kids had gradually trickled down to major holidays, and then for only an hour at most. Clearly, all she loved was Daniel's money arriving in her bank account on the first of every month.

He thought of reporting her extortion to the cops, but since he was, in fact, three months late on his court-ordered alimony, that could backfire in a...heartbeat. He could lose custody.

After a couple hits of CBDay to clear his head and help him focus, he dove deep into the weeds on the defunct software embedded in his chest.

Breaking into the source through the app was child's play; it was like those code monkeys didn't even try to lock it up properly. Line by line, he traced the master loop through every subroutine with admin privileges. He stayed up all night looking for the lines that could kill him at the whim of his ex with a single flick of her little finger.

Compared to the sophisticated hard and soft code he worked with every day, this thing was really nothing more than a glorified plastic RV water pump, except made of titanium with a few sensors and a wireless internet layer. But there was one ugly block of dense gobbledygook that was obviously encrypted—some kind of digital rights management, perhaps? Then his mechanically pumped blood ran cold when he realized it was likely something along the lines of the notorious "jack-in-the-box" installed in all new cars these days, the ones that enabled the lender to remotely disable your motor if you missed one too many payments. DRM like this was borderline military grade and reportedly impenetrable by mere mortals like him.

There was, of course, no tech support he could contact at the extinct company that built his heart and, predictably, not a soul at the foreign mega-corp that had subsumed HeartUS would respond with anything but a fluffy form letter. They didn't even have the decency to offer him a discount on a replacement. He definitely couldn't afford to hire an attorney to sue the bastards, so he joined a forum for faux-heart transplant recipients and dug deep into its massive post history, scanning for anything about the remote management code that now threatened his life.

After a long night of dredging through endless sob stories and opinionated sludge, Daniel sent a direct message from the BeatOfLife forum directory to someone who seemed to have a clue.

"Hi-ho Cardi0Silver! I read your posts on the forum and wondered if we could talk IRL. I have a remote management issue with my HeartUS unit model

9.1 and I am willing to pay you to help me debug it. I am an engineer but this encrypted DRM shit is way above my pay grade. Please DM me ASAP."

Three hours later, his phone pinged with a DM notification. Almost dropping it on the kitchen tile as he was making breakfast for the kids, he read the response: "I can help. US$500 equivalent in bitcoin per hour, not negotiable. Send burner phone number in alpha text and I call you."

Daniel thought: *For that kind of money, Cardi0Silver better be a fucking genius—not like an Apple Store genius but a REAL genius.* But what other choice did he have? This shady, anonymous, paranoid, barely English-speaking hacker was a risk he could not afford, but was apparently his only viable lifeline. *Live free or die* had taken on a whole new meaning.

⌘

"You need tools," said Cardi0Silver in a thick Russian accent. "Create one-time email at seenoevil.sputnix.ru and send to me then I send you files. Do it now and I wait."

Daniel did as he was told. The attachments he received through the wonky webmail screen were two barebones x86 executables that his new friend said would access his heart's circuit directly via bluetooth, bypassing his phone app entirely. As directed, he launched heartUS9Xdecrypt.exe, after which Cardi0Silver walked him through the decryption, then asked for screenshots of the displayed codes.

"You are ok! Same version in me. Now launch heartUS9Xadmin.exe then type DISABLE SECONDARY

ACCESS in query field, all cap. When screen displays SECONDARY ACCESS DISABLED close apps and you are done. No remote management now through phone app allowed except from primary which is you. 49 minutes so send US$409 equivalent bitcoin to sensay@domagrafix.ru now. Hide and encrypt apps they are not legal. Violate DMCA. Delete all our text and destroy burner."

Daniel replied, "That's it? How will I know it worked?"

"Worked for me. I have same model inside. Be happy! You are free man!"

Daniel paid Cardi0Silver and prayed that it worked. His HeartUS phone app showed no changes or new notifications, so he figured that he wouldn't know for sure without some kind of test, a test that could kill him. He would have to poke the bear.

⌘

"Sorry Ariel, but I cannot pay you anything until after business picks up in a month or so. Perhaps you could help out with the kids while I work 18 hours a day? If that's too damn much to ask, then you do what you have to do. Incidentally, if you kill me, custody automatically reverts to you."

It was an unsubtle broadside, but Ariel was a pretty dull tool and probably wouldn't understand anything less—it had to sting. She was either going to stop his heart or not, and he had only the word of some random Russian dude to have faith in now.

Daniel vaped himself to sleep with CBDream as he waited for the worst. *There are times when all you can fucking do is wait*, he mused with his brain bathed in legal substances. Either he would take the kids to school in the morning, or Child Services would.

Woke up, got out of bed, dragged a comb across my head, he sang to himself. So far, his heart was still beating, so he performed his morning ablutions, made bacon and eggs and toast, then got his two beautiful, innocent children ready for school. There was the usual running around looking for backpacks and bears and other necessities, but that's nominal. He hesitated as he got in the car—*What if I keel over while driving them?*—but resolved to stick with their morning routine and just drive, albeit at the slowest legal speed through town, avoiding the expressway.

Back at home, he got right to work after telling himself to stop thinking about all this madness. *You can't let the terrorists win!* he thought.

Back in his bedroom office, eating a sandwich as he stared at waveforms on his screens, he resolved to keep calm and carry on, as the old blitz posters advised. They're a cliché now, but still a damn worthwhile thing to remember in trying times. It became for him a kind of mantra. What the hell else could he do?

"She may still have the power to break my heart for good. But at least I have a heart to break."

— • • • —

The Peace Weapon

"Turn the key!"

"I can't do it! We don't know what will happen…"

"Bundy's men have breached the east gate. We have no choice now, luv. Turn the fucking key!"

She turned it with her eyes closed, silently injecting an invisible packet of re-engineered particles into the collider. There was no explosion, no flash, no sensation at all—just a barely audible click.

⌘

High above the White Mountains straddling California and Nevada, twenty five miles up a steep grade, lies the ancient bristlecone pine preserve. Driving on US395, turn east at Lone Pine, drive up the mountain until your car overheats, and you're there. You are in the moonscape realm of the oldest living things on the planet.

Nearly a mile below, Methuselah Station was built in total secrecy. Officially, it is referred to as Federal Research Area 42, but those on the inside just called it the hole. There are cloaked entrances on either side of the mountain, but the east gate was a hundred miles from the nearest town so nearly everyone used the west gate in California. Livermore and Stanford were 45 minutes away via VTOL shuttle.

In this enormous cavern was erected a clone of the CERN supercollider, but it was not an exact duplicate. The suffocating EU safety protocols were entirely ignored, and other significant mods were made, not the least of which was access to an energy reserve with over six times the power of its weak European sister. If needed, southern California and all of Nevada could be shut down to feed the beast. They hadn't tried this, but the option was there.

⌘

"Isn't it beautiful, Paul!"

She had climbed the highest crag at the observation turnout near the top of the mountain. The view of the Sierras was breathtaking and made her feel like she was seeing across half the state, though it was barely a couple hundred miles on a good day. The only thing that spoiled the view was the curvature of the Earth and the air quality du jour.

"Yes, Linda. Spectacular by any measure. But I'm afraid my acrophobia insists that I retreat a bit. By the way, shouldn't we be getting back down before the storm? You must have noticed the stratocumulus cluster coming in from the southwest. Shall I sat the Lone Pine Cafe for a res?"

"Sure, but no need for sat charges. There is still good old CDMA up here, so save your money for the wine!"

"Roger that, luv."

He scrabbled down fifty feet to the parking area and made the call on his hiking phone, a battered old

Moto flip. Of course it worked—she was always right about mountain things. She grew up a few hundred miles from here, which in the west was like a quick run to the liquor store to any easterner.

Down the mountain, the cafe was busier than they expected, considering the season. The waiter recognized Linda and took them below into the wine cave to make their selection. When the waiter left them to browse, and now confident of the lack of RF surveillance, she opened up.

"Paul, what the hell are we really doing down there? I'm not complaining, I love my job, but things are getting kinda weird in the hole. People don't really talk anymore. Everyone is looking over their shoulder and it really sucks."

He thought about all the NDAs he'd signed and the severe sanctions that he could suffer if he broke them. He knew the direction of the research, but could not bring himself to offer more to her than a general outline. This pained him so much he had to consciously relax his facial muscles lest he reveal his stress.

"Right. There is some talk of testing full-power mode with some experimental particles from the lab, but I'm not really sure of anything." He hoped that would suffice, but of course it didn't—Linda could always smell a half-truth.

"Well how the hell could we do that without shouting our presence out to the entire western US?"

"I imagine a cover story would be needed after shutting off power to 60 million people. But it's above my pay-grade to know anything more, really."

"Right", she said, slightly drawing out the vowel. He knew he would have to tell her what he knew or he would sleep on their lumpy old couch tonight, and that just wasn't going to happen, federal prison be damned. *The things we do for love*, he sang in his head.

"Are you sure this cellar is secure? I'd prefer a proper Faraday cage, or perhaps something under a million tons of rock instead of a crumbling old desert bar."

"I know *just* the place. Let's eat!"

She told him about an old silver mine on the east side of the mountain. Raised in Nevada by a geological engineer father, she'd been all over what most people would consider a flyover wasteland, but she knew better.

"Let's requisition a rover and drive there Saturday morning."

"On what pretext, luv?" Paul said with a smirk.

"Perimeter security research, of course!"

⌘

The scenery was beautiful in the way all deserts are beautiful, like staring out over the ocean. The desolation and lack of color, combined with the seemingly endless straight stretches of road encouraged a kind of zen state…zen with lots of strong coffee and sandwiches. They talked of ordinary things—parents, siblings, movies, the new lunar base—avoiding their little chat in the wine cave.

In quiet moments, Paul ruminated on what he would tell her. He wasn't privy to everything, but he knew enough to understand that his superiors were edging toward something groundbreaking in physics. Not necessarily Trinity-class, but definitely something risky, and risks like that are only taken when there is a threat accelerating the deliberate time frame of science. The fact that it was being developed in total secrecy made it all the more likely it would quietly fail under that mountain—how, exactly, do you put *that* on your résumé? *So what have you been working on for the last two years, Paul? Oh, I was perfecting my golf swing and playing a lot of billiards—you know, practical physics!*

"There it is! Hang a left just ahead. Slow down, hot rod: it turns into dirt right after the cattle guard," she said. Satnavs were useless to her out here, not because they didn't work but because once you get off the highway, most of these roads have no name. The damn things just start badgering you to *Resume the route…Recalculating…Resume the route…*until you shut the stupid thing off, but only after a few salty words casting aspersions on that particular robot's lineage.

"Okay. About four miles ahead, as I recall," she said over the rumble of the rover's metal torsion wheels. "We used to hunt for gemstones out here. Bagged some big opals at the base of those hills."

Paul parked in a clearing where a small encampment used to be, they got out, slung on their daypacks, and walked a few hundred yards to the entrance to the mine. Torches on, they trudged down a few hundred feet until they found a high-ceilinged cavern littered with rusted iron junk.

"We can't go any deeper. A bunch of miners died in collapses until they finally closed the shaft. But there is still loads of silver above—they were just afraid to go after it. Too risky."

Stopping here was fine with Paul. He felt claustrophobic. *People must have been a lot shorter two centuries ago*, he thought.

Linda said, "Okay. What's the deal at 42? It's just no fun to work there anymore."

"Um, right," he said, plopping himself down on a rock next to her. "I already told you most of what I know; here's the rest: The experimental particles are expected to have a mild effect on the human brain, limited to an estimated two kilometers in diameter around the collider. Don't freak out, the effect is intended to be positive. It's not a weapon per se, but there *is* a small possibility that things may go, um…a bit sideways, shall we say? Are we human Guinea pigs down in the hole? Absolutely. Could a few dozen others within the bubble's perimeter be affected during the test? Yes.

"The best way I've heard it described is as a 'peace weapon'. Basically, it's a two kilometer wide drug that gently and safely induces contemplation and self-awareness. We just don't know precisely how long the effect will last. There is no way to test it under low power."

She looked at him like she had just seen pigs fly over his head.

"Very funny, limey-boy. Very funny. You forgot about the wizards and the elves…"

"I am not making this up, luv. Think about the applications. Ending battles before they start. Calming civil unrest and domestic police actions like riot control. Inducing real peace wherever it's needed and *only* where it's needed. It's the ultimate non-weapon, the opposite of a gun."

She still held that look of utter disbelief, waiting for the punchline.

"Hey, *you* asked me and that's what I know," he said with the look and body language of resignation.

"You're serious? You can't be serious. Honestly, Paul, that is the single craziest fucking thing I have ever heard."

"Yeah, I get that. I kind of freaked out too, at first. Look, luv: I'm not trying to talk you into it. If you have to run, then run. But at least consider this: I am in daily contact with the people behind this test, and they are, quite literally, the smartest humans on this bloody planet—the best of the best. They think this thing can work and that the risk of failure is overbalanced by the potentially incalculable benefit to our species. Millions of lives saved using a temporary intervention with zero casualties, scalable from a single house to a small city. It's brilliant, but a bit scary too.

"Sure, the ick factor is huge. But the lives that could be protected from barbaric emotions, all the pointless battles stopped in their tracks…isn't that worth investigating on a relatively small scale? I'm not saying I'm all in, and honestly I don't think anybody upstairs is either. But you and I are *scientists*. We take risks testing our hypotheses, our hunches—'*Risk is our business'*, as Captain Kirk said, right? Do you really believe the ultimate anti-weapon is not worth one hyperlocal experiment?"

She just gave him a pained look as they walked out of the mine in silence.

"A peace bomb, hmm?" she said as the rover approached the east gate. "What could *possibly* go wrong?"

He decided it would be best to keep his mouth shut and just get back to their shared quarters in the hole. She was either staying or leaving; nothing he could say tonight would make any difference now.

⌘

Just as they pulled up to the cloak, they were instantly surrounded by a squad of MPs. Linda and Paul reflexively raising their hands with half a dozen black rifles pointed at their heads. Both of the rover's front doors were flung open and commands were barked. They slowly presented their IDs as ordered, then the rover was searched and deep scanned. After the sergeant got approval in his earjack, they were waved through the gate to the motor pool.

Once they were on the elevator, she said, "What the fuck is happening, Paul?"

"I have no idea. Security breach? Radiation leak? The colonel has his knickers in a twist because his A's lost?"

The corridors on their level were empty. Back in their quarters, Linda poured two stiff bourbons and put them on the coffee table.

"You'd think they would have sent out a priority memo or something. This is just creepy," she said with a frightened half-smile he had never seen on her face before.

"Our orders are to shelter in place and await further instructions. I'm calling upstairs and you should too. Be cool, luv."

All they could get from their superiors was that Methuselah Station was on yellow alert. Someone had apparently leaked to the radical right-wing Bundy clan, whose compound is in nearby Bunkerville Nevada, details of an imminent experiment involving a massive power blackout to the southwestern US.

"Well that's just bloody lovely," said Paul wearing a mock smile. "I read there are known Bundy enclaves in southern Cali east of LA as well. Somebody upstairs bloody better have called in a division of Marines from Pendleton. We are surrounded by those nutters."

"What are they going to do if they shoot their way in?" She said. "Take us all hostage?"

"These bozos are fiercely anti-science and anti-government. They could C4 the collider, then out us all as members of a secret government conspiracy—which, to be fair, we kind of *are*."

"Fuck. *Fuck* those fucking fuckers. Pass the whiskey."

⌘

An hour and a half passed with no news from on high.

"I wish we had one of your goddamn peace bombs right about now, Paulie."

"Well uh…we sort of do. The whole sequence is in the computers upstairs and ready to go. Only takes one level 6 operator and an assistant in the control room, and I am a level 6, so HA! Maybe this time *England* saves *America*!"

"When did you get level 6, you magnificent limey bastard?"

"I was going to tell you on the drive back but, you know…"

"Well then fuck it, Paulie. If barbarians are at the gate, we need to do whatever we can to protect the place. I think it's in our employment contracts…"

"Are you bloody serious? Now it's *your* turn to talk crazy, eh?"

"What the hell. Let's just go up there and see who's guarding the crown jewels…like right now."

He looked at her for a long, measured moment, the whiskey haze fading fast. She was dead serious. He stood up and struck a dramatic pose: "Begone, pale cast of thought! Once more into the breach, and so on!" He held out his hand and said, "Let's *science* those redhats."

⌘

Empty hallways and an empty stairwell, all the way to the control room. *Where is everybody?* He thought, then chuckled at his lame Fermi paradox reference. *Shit, I'm getting sicklied o'er…*

She looked at him and said, "Focus, man. Focus!"

Paul stared into the eyecam and the door clicked. The control room was empty, so they strolled in like they owned the place.

"So we just sit here until we hear gunfire, right? Then what do we do?" she asked.

"I log in, bring up the master test page, set the power to, say, 10%, and start the collider sequence. Twenty seconds later, the gray ready light will turn red. You stand at the yellow panel and prepare to turn the keyswitch marked ENGAGE, of course. After that, we're committed; a sudden halt will cause instability, so there's no turning back."

"I feel sick."

"It's just the whiskey wearing off, luv. We've run simulations and everything printed nominal."

Then they felt and heard four consecutive explosions, followed by muffled overlapping automatic weapons fire—nothing like a machine gun to sober you up fast. Paul reached over to the adjacent screen and tapped the security cam tab, bringing up a dozen view options. He chose INTERIOR GATE VESTIBULE - EAST and saw four views bustling with armed men in civilian clothing. He couldn't tell if the MPs were returning fire or not—it was total chaos.

He started the collider sequence with a tap. The gray ready light turned red.

"Turn the key!"

"I can't do it! We don't know what will happen..."

"Bundy's men have breached the east gate. We have no choice now, luv. Turn the fucking key!"

She turned it with her eyes closed, silently injecting an invisible packet of re-engineered particles into the collider. There was no explosion, no flash, no sensation at all—just a barely audible click.

Paul watched the insurgents in the vestibule cams as they stopped firing and slowly lowered their rifles. In a second, the battle went silent. The combatants looked at each other, their wills suddenly puzzled. The assault just stopped.

Linda opened her eyes and looked at Paul. He said, "The good news is, they've ceased fire. The bad news is I forgot to reduce the power slider to 10% before you turned the key, so we don't know how far the pulse has spread—the default is 100%. I don't know why, but frankly, I don't really care right now. Do you?

"She smiled and said, "I don't care either. I was terrified but now I'm cool as early summer rain. Haven't felt this good since I don't know when. You?"

"Absolutely. Isn't it wonderful, luv?"

⌘

The smartest people in the world could not have predicted the aftermath of the first "peace bomb" test. The 100% power blast reached over 3000 kilometers in diameter, reaching across nearly 60% of the US, a huge swath of Canada, and half of Mexico. Planes in the airspace above and ships at sea in the Pacific and Gulf were affected; even scuba divers in the deep felt it. And not a soul was hurt, not a single traffic accident was caused, and there were zero violent crimes committed within the pulse zone. In Mexico, even the bloody northern cartels cooled their jets for weeks. Everyone within the bubble just felt...fine. It lasted for nearly two months for those closest to the station, gradually ebbing away for everyone affected to varying degrees based on their proximity to the hole.

Washington claimed the test was designed to calibrate quantum target predictions for orbit-to-ground, non-nuclear projectiles. Nothing to see here, people. Typical DOD stuff, the kind that keeps us all safe at night. The mass calming effect was an "unintended consequence of a massive power surge in the lab" and those responsible would be held to account.

No one bought the cover story; even Fox News called bullshit, and every Fox mini-me echoed them. But there was so much positive news fallout that within a day all those perpetually grouchy extremists were quickly drowned out.

Fewer than one hundred people knew anything about their work down in the hole, and most of them could not even see a tiny glimpse of the implications of their work. As in all organizations, eighty-five percent were useful fools, ten percent were paper-pushing managerial types, and the remainder were certifiable geniuses who thought they knew exactly what they were doing. What ultimately happened on the ground proved it was not in anyone's vocabulary of possibilities that this massively beneficial effect would be so widespread, so undeniably *good* for everyone affected and those who yearned to be.

Of course, there was nearly unanimous condemnation of America's new "happy bomb" from folks outside the effect bubble and those, predictably, were mostly eastern US coastal media outlets. The few scattered complaints from inside the bubble were from the usual cadre of ultraconservatives who loved nothing more than to whine about government intrusion.

As for top-secret Methuselah Station, the cat was out of the proverbial bag. Camps formed at both entrances with thousands of protesters as well as double that number begging to be near ground zero for test number two. It looked like a civil disaster waiting to happen, but somehow it never escalated to violence.

The world had changed once again in a nanosecond, but unlike the Trinity test in 1945, this change could benefit us all.

⌘

Back in their quarters, Linda said, "What do you think happens next?"

"I don't know, luv, and no one's talking. Everything is locked up bloody tight. Bundy's goon squad must have had someone inside the hole to find out about the test, probably someone fairly high up. All they needed to irritate them enough to attack was to know that a secret government facility was about to siphon off all their power for unknown reasons. Big science, big government, big secrets—it was like waving red flags at their bull."

"I went through two interviews—pretty brutal. I meant what happens with the peace bomb?"

"All that is way above our pay gra—"

"Bullshit, Paulie! They'll shrink it down to a tactical weapon and use it to neutralize enemies."

"They will have to figure out how to stuff a 27 kilometer-wide supercollider into a truck-size box or a cargo plane first. That's going to take a bit of work."

"Yeah, but they'll eventually do it and they'll deploy it. And the race is on…"

"That's depressing, that is, but also kind of comforting: a peace race? Doesn't sound too bad to me."

Exasperated, Linda said, "I love you, Paul, but sometimes you are *so* naive. They will find a way to use this against innocent people, total non-combatants. And if there was a way to make the effect permanent…"

"Um, *theoretically*, that is feasible," Paul interrupted. "It's bloody mind control, so no one is seriously proposing…"

"Holy shit!" she exclaimed. "Bomb the world with peace? That's *insane*."

"Who said anything about the world? Just the bad guys."

"But Paulie, what if *they* get there first and, to them, *we* are the bad guys?"

— • • • —

Hot for 'Naut

NASA did not see it coming. ROSCOSMOS almost certainly did, because Russians. JAXA was blindsided and terribly embarrassed, as the Japanese often are. India didn't know what to do and quietly deferred to the Americans for guidance; their manned space program was the youngest and most politically fragile as yet another conflict with Pakistan over Kashmir heated up. The Chinese? The apparatchiks at CMSA would never admit it, even if a taikonaut did the dirty deed in the middle of Tiananmen Square.

There were prostitutes of both genders in orbit, on all three moon bases, and possibly en route to the fledgeling SpaceX Mars base at Hellas Planitia. These were not your garden variety whores, but trained agents with a clear mission: accumulate kompromat on humanity's greatest heroes, all living and working in what boils down to a bunch of cramped, smelly RV trailers in space with hundreds of cameras and sensors capturing everything they do, every second of every day, right down to each and every heartbeat.

Civilian billionaires built the space tourism industry by laying their personal fortunes, and their own asses, on the line. Six years after the first suborbital show-flights, such weightless and pointless journeys were now weekly self-promo photo ops for the elite. What better way for these rich jerks to lord their superiority over the huddled masses stuck at the bottom of the gravity well than to fly over them at twenty nine thousand kilometers per hour, twirling around in microgravity with their mediagenic PR directors—all with goofy grins plastered on their faces? The ultimate class statement had been achieved: kings, presidents, dictators...all passé now. If these new masters of the universe could have pissed out of their designer spacesuits on all of the rest of us, they bloody well would have.

In retrospect, this turn of global fortunes and influence was utterly predictable: trillion dollar corps, and the wannabe astronauts running them, were now in charge. They bought and sold entire economies with pocket change, encountering only mock resistance from the impoverished governments of what was left of the inhabitable world. Politicians whose next election was bought and paid for in advance by the megacorps, using the darkest of dark monies, did as they "thought best for the people", while the little-boys-in-big-kid-spacesuits asked amongst themselves, '*We already rule this rock, so how do we rule the final fucking frontier?*'

⌘

The Flight Director burst into the Chief Astronaut's office across the hall from his. "Where is John Glenn when we need him? Yuri Gagarin? Neil Armstrong? Valentina Tereshkova? Sally Ride? *Real* fucking astronauts! I'd kill for a young Chuck Yeager to fly up there to punch some sense into these whiners!"

"They don't make 'em like that anymore, boss," said Stanley Austin, sitting in his Aeron sipping the usual burnt Starbucks from downstairs. He'd been flying that chair for four years since surviving the Clavius disaster, while dealing with a human disaster or two right here in Houston every goddamned day.

"Never should have given them new guys Instagrams or whatever the hell kids use this week," said Flight.

"We don't call them 'guys' anymore."

"Hell, Stan. You know what I mean," growled Flight.

Turns out space travelers were, unsurprisingly, human. Put men and women in a metal box for months and they are going to find a way to have sex with each other. Most 'nauts were happily married with kids, but as with business travelers in Vegas, things change in the wild—what happened in space stayed in space for years, but that was many millions of kilometers in the rear view ago.

⌘

Dr. Austin had flown to Luna three times, building humanity's first credible base on that dusty rock. He was on-base when a SpaceX supply ship crashed sideways a hundred meters off the landing pad, blowing four of his people into the vacuum and half the base into blackened rubble. After getting the remaining seven people and himself into a another lander, he vowed never to return to the black. Space travel became an addiction for most 'nauts, but not for him, not anymore. He just wanted to stand on the big blue marble and not think too much about what he had seen out there.

Now he and Flight had to deal daily with stupid people tricks in space. Everyone knew that mixing "influencers" with real scientist-explorers was a recipe for failure, but popular engagement and ad dollars paid the majority of their salaries now. NASA bowed to fiscal pressure from DC to let the insufferable showbiz kids making movies of themselves into the ISS and then into shuttles to Luna; it had been a constant, distracting headache since day one. None of the veteran 'nauts or ground crews could stand the shallow little creeps, but they had to make the best of it; American space travel had become a government/commercial enterprise and that's just the way it had to be—it was either that or let the Chinese take the high ground away from them, and that just was not going to happen.

And now, of course, it was *Real Influencers in Space*. The situation was ripe for exploitation and abuse, all dished out daily on all the streaming services. *'We reached for the stars and ended up babysitting George Clooney's beautiful brats,'* Stanley often thought to himself.

It wasn't just NASA dealing with this crap; assholenaut culture creeped into all the spacefaring nation's vehicles and stations within a year of their domination of American television. The viewing public came to expect microgravity entertainments as older celebrities joined the freefall fun and games. Tom Hanks' first flight was the most watched livecast in history, outgrossing the 1969 Apollo 11 landing by a factor of four.

Government space stations and SpaceX's Starship shuttles had gotten mighty crowded. Everyone at NASA knew it was time to build commercial LEO stations and eventually a civilian moon base. Of course, Elon Musk was five years ahead of them. He had been working on both projects for a decade, as a quiet side play while creating a permanent Mars base. Compared to that, building a simple orbital hotel was trivial, so they started on it, then announced their moon hotel project. Science was expensive, but rows of pressurized steel cans with a view was relatively cheap for the world's first multi-trillionaire. After acquiring both Apple and Google, Musk's juggernaut was unstoppable.

⌘

"Stan, get up here now! We've got a problem."

Stanley heard the fear in Flight's voice and bolted upstairs as fast as his 1G legs would propel him.

"Some net-hole has videos showing two of your people fornicating with civilians. We have sample clips —it's for real."

"What? Who?"

"Walt on the ISS and Sara at Clavius," said Flight through gritted teeth.

"What do they want?"

"Whaddya think they want, doc? What else do these little pricks want. Money!"

"Damn! This has to be a setup. I know both of them quite well and they are simply not the types who..."

"Fuck in space with civies half their age, in multi-angle 8K? Jesus..."

"These...civilians—we must know who they are. Could they be foreign agents?"

"My thoughts exactly and DC thinks so too. They are all over this right now, but what the *hell* are we supposed to do from here? There's just no way this works out in our favor— no fucking way."

Stanley ran through every scenario his shocked brain could concoct; perhaps Flight was right: they should pay and pray.

Later that morning, it was determined that the two civies involved were American born, but the fact that the blackmails were explicitly for both the orbital and lunar events indicated a coordinated threat, probably foreign. Of course, their astronomical demands were to be paid in untraceable Bitcoin. DC was waffling in their guidance of this delicate matter, as their stated policy is to never negotiate with terrorists, as these blackmailers were now considered.

The two NASA 'nauts named were mid-level military officers, a newly minted Space Force captain and a decorated Navy commander. Both their careers could be ended if the videos got out, and the black eye NASA would receive could set the mission back years.

"What if we just let them release the videos and ride out the storm?" said Stanley. "We minimize the threat as a cheap trick and shrug it off. It's entrapment, sure, but is this really a national security risk?"

This suggestion landed in the conference room with a thud.

"We could check with our counterparts in Russia, China, Japan, and India to see if they've had their people threatened," Stanley continued.

"And tip our hand? Are you nuts?" barked Flight, who was in an unusually foul mood.

"Gentlemen, we have already made inquiries to all the spacefaring states and all report incidents in the last ten days, with similar demands in similarly worded statements," said Ida Menkin, an envoy from the FBI. "The bureau believes this is clearly a coordinated threat and should be treated as an act of terrorism."

"You've *got* to be kidding me!" howled Flight.

"Sadly, I am not kidding. But this does effectively rule out a spacefaring nation as the culprit. As such, we have concentrated our efforts on a private operation, global in scope," said Agent Menkin.

"So all they want is a couple hundred million to make it all go away? No other demands? Hell, it takes more than that to get half a dozen of their—*operatives*, shall we call them?—into space riding on our damn spacecraft. It doesn't make sense!" Flight was in fine form today. How the old man ever got posted to a job requiring the coolest of heads was a total mystery, but with the director on medical leave, Flight was running the show.

"Look: these operatives are social media stars. A billion people paid for *Friends* in space with their eyeballs and their subscriptions. What if the novelty of Ross and Rachel goofing off in microgravity is wearing off and this whole sex scandal is just a drastic bid for more likes?" said Stanley, getting a little worked up himself after his previous comments were dismissed so abruptly.

The conference room went quiet for a long moment.

Agent Menkin stood up and said, "The FBI and our spacefaring nation counterparts around the world believe this to be an international security threat. At the very least, it is a serious crime committed by a multi-national conspiracy."

"Wait just a goddamn minute," Flight seethed. "These are *our* men and women up there, targeted and entrapped by space sluts. Are you suggesting, Stan, that we just let their careers die so a hundred million teeny-boppers can have a laugh? Fuck that! *Not on my watch.*"

Stanley stood up and said, "If we just cuff these operatives and send them all home to trial, their handlers will release the tapes. If we get out ahead of this scam, we can make these bozos a laughingstock *and* not pay them a dime. We get the Pentagon to forgive our people due to their entrapment. It'll be a PR nightmare, of course, but it *will* pass."

"The bureau will not…"

Flight roared, "The bureau does not have jurisdiction on my spacecraft and my stations—NASA does, and *I'm* in charge here." The room went silent again. Visibly cooling down a little, Flight's voice approached nominal. "As much as I hate to disgrace the greatest space agency on and off Earth, I think Stan is right: the risk is manageable and we can protect our people—and bag the idiots who thought they could catch us with our pants floating around our ankles. I want the president and joint chiefs on the line in ten minutes. I can sell this, and they can sell it to all the other nations under threat."

⌘

And sold it he did, the magnificent bastard. President Buttigieg appointed him to be NASA's director and Stanley was made the new Flight. They rounded up all the operatives—soon to be referred to in the media as "Hot For 'Naut"—and shipped them back down the well to face charges. As Stanley predicted, it was a coordinated publicity stunt that blew over as fast as any common terrestrial sex scandal does. Every 'naut involved was exonerated, except, predictably, the taikonauts, whose whereabouts remain unknown months after their somber earthfall. The CCP has, as always, zero sense of humor and does not appreciate the slightest criticism from anyone. You'd think the most populous nation on Earth would understand a thing or two about people having sex, but saving Dear Leader's face was more important than saving the careers of three 'nauts. Plenty more where they came from.

The final frontier. To boldly go. Whoop de do.

— • • • —

NeuroType

[Desert figure, sun behind with long shadow ahead, walking slow with head down]

[VO Billy Bob Thornton] "It's a lonely world. An endless stream of people who just don't get you."

[Nonspecific multiracial woman's pained face hovering on the verge of tears]

"Now there is a safe space where everyone thinks just like you, where everyone understands what you like and how you think. Where no one will judge you for who you are naturally—for who you *really are*."

[Desert woman's face dissolves to a serene garden filled with smiling people]

"Welcome to NeuroType™. One simple, painless DNA test you can do in your safe space will generate your NeuroType™ number. Then, once you are connected with millions of people who think just like you do, you can share as much, or as little, as you wish, at your own pace. The possibilities are endless and guaranteed to be emotionally safe or your money back."

[Closeup of two gender-nonspecific people facing in profile against the sunrise]

"We are NeuroType™. Join us and see what you've been missing your whole life."

Lise shut her laptop, tears streaming unevenly down her cheeks. Stifling her sobs, she stared at her window facing the brick wall across the alley and tried not to make any noise that could wake her boyfriend. He just wouldn't understand—ever.

She opened her laptop, filled out the three-screen questionnaire, and paid the $99 fee plus another $19 for morning test kit delivery. With any luck, Brandon would be in his closet office with headphones on when FedEx arrived.

Lise's initial impression of her "cognate graph", as the company called her match cohort, was promising. She received nine PMs within an hour of going live on the service, even though her profile was sparse. The livephoto she uploaded was but a brief glimpse of her face that quickly turned away from the camera. No physical stats, no age, no gender pref, no relationship status, just her city and a bland "Hi I'm new here" message. She had been edating her entire adult life and knew the drill; she was not going to fall for any of the usual bullshit from anyone.

"Lise? Can you hear me?"

"Um, hi, yes. Dana?

"Yes, it's me. I saw you pop up on my graph and was *so* relieved that you identify as female. The males I've exchanged with have been… rather gloomy. Have you noticed this?"

"Honestly, you are the first call I have accepted."

"So what are you into, Lise? I love 1970's singer-songwriters, libraries, hard sci-fi, and Asian food. You?"

"All the above! Jackson Browne rules, early or late."

"He's my fave too! Too bad he's dead. Wanna get some lunch?"

Lise paused, pretending to answer the door for a delivery. She needed to process; this was all happening too fast for her.

"That sounds good," said Lise after taking a breath. "There is a lovely Korean place on 49th near the library..."

"Sweet! Noon?"

"Yes. See you there."

It was a perfect date. She'd been with women before in college, but none of them were anything like Dana. They spent the day in Dana's little apartment, talking about books, watching old Star Trek episodes, and making love. She'd never felt more comfortable with anyone.

After three more secret assignations with Dana, she was ready to leave Brandon and his stupid crap. At last, she was in love with a soulmate.

Lise and Dana started going to bespoke parties arranged by NeuroType. Only Type 16 members were allowed, a diverse collection of literally like-minded people. They were always fun and lacked the drama of parties Lise had wasted far too much time on before. She never felt challenged or threatened—it was just perfect.

"What have you done to my Lise!" bellowed Brandon, his face twisted into a fierce simian snarl. He had crashed the door to the private party room and everyone turned to face him.

Lise, stunned, said nothing, but Dana stood up and yelled, "Nothing that wasn't already there, you brute! *Get out!*"

After NeuroType's private security subdued Brandon, tased him unconscious, and dragged him to the street, Lise and Dana sat down and talked it out. Other T16s came by to commiserate and support her; seems this kind of reaction from exes was a common occurrence among her cohort.

"He is so angry. In a way, I don't blame him—I kind of took away his dream," Lise said.

"What dream?"

"He wanted to get married and start a family with me."

"What a fucking idiot," snorted Dana. "Children are for normies, not people like us."

Lise felt numb and said nothing. She loved Dana and adored the idea of spending the rest of her days surrounded by her and other T16s and maybe even branching out to NeuroType-approved adjacent types someday. But even as she thought this, she felt hollowed out in a way she'd never felt before.

"I'm going to see him. Security broke two ribs and fractured an arm. He's at General."

"Fucker deserved everything he got for breaking our perimeter," scowled Dana.

"I loved him before I loved you. He deserves a visit at the very least."

Dana sniffed and turned back to her book.

No matter how she tried to explain to him how she felt and how she had changed, Brandon was beyond emotional reach. He was shut down and inconsolable, so Lise went back to Dana's apartment, entering as quietly as she could.

Her newfound cocoon of love, safety, and sameness was all-consuming. Being with only like-minded people was an irresistibly powerful opiate that alleviated her loneliness and alienation. If she had to cancel everyone she knew to avoid the inevitable friction of real life, so be it. This new reality was almost too good to be true and that was enough for her.

— ••• —

Re: The Solitaire™

Re: The Solitaire™

Sent: 7/30/2026 11:49 PM

To: chb@marcom.atavista.com

From: dtm@marcom.atavista.com

Imagine a smartphone that zigs when all the others zag: Presenting The Solitaire™, the ultimate slacker's phone that shamelessly mimics Apple and Android devices while offering essentially none of their annoying functionality. The Solitaire™ doesn't connect to anything except cell towers and just barely accomplishes that. Need an excuse to not receive a call? Just leave your Solitaire™ under a Chipotle wrapper and you will never get that call.

The Solitaire™ is self-contained and fiercely proud of its independence. With no irritating Bluetooth settings or fiddly cables to connect, The Solitaire™ doesn't even know that personal computers or the cloud exist and doesn't really give a shit about either.

Let those millions of lemmings obsessed with trendy aesthetics buy their fancy iDevices, if they can find one to buy. You'll never wait in line with a hundred sweaty nerds to buy your Solitaire™, 100% guaranteed. Plodding mediocrity shall prevail over the spark of innovation yet again—the people have spoken!

Imagine the ad campaign:

"The Solitaire™. The first smartphone that combines ignorance with indifference."

The mob chants rhythmically, *"I don't know and I don't care!"*

You see, The Solitaire™ has exactly zero fucks to give because it uses SolipsOS™, an operating system that uses the universally beloved metaphor of the Solitaire card game to represent calls, texts, apps, alarms, alert boxes—everything. SolipsOS™ lets you run your smartphone like most people run their lives: like a totally futile game. Go ahead and shuffle that fat stack of shit-to-do items—who fucking cares? Which double-booked appointments should you attend? New game! And when you occasionally do something right, all the cards fly around leaving psychedelic trails all over your screen.

It's a great time to be alive, isn't it?

Life is random, messy, and tacky, so why shouldn't our smartphones reflect this? Most calls are spam or bad news, most texts are from people asking you to do shit for them, all appointments can be rescheduled, and fewer than 10% of people keep lists of anything. People don't really want to be organized, they just want to have fun. Let's give 'em what they want: The Solitaire™!

The Solitaire™ is available at these fine stores: Wal-Mart, McDonalds, 7-11, Jiffy Lube, and Taco Bell.

— • • • —

The Value Of Nothing

"Abort, Joey," barked the professor. "It's too big a risk. We may now have all the evidence we need to charge them at the Geneva world…"

"Right," Joey said sarcastically. "Two years in court while they regroup? Cut off one head and two more appear? We will never have this chance again to crush them and their machines." He thought to himself *'There is a tide..'*

⌘

Halfway up the western slope of Northern California's Sierra Nevada range, in a place called Shingle Springs, was a nondescript, four-unit office park. The professor had built her eleven person consulting business there, mostly because the region's ISP was literally next door to her office. She ran a website for the business, as well as archive sites for all of her previous ventures into tech publishing, and her many academic papers for those interested in such arcana. She liked the hands-on control over her data that she had just one door away. Of course, one could get slightly faster net speeds several hundred miles north-northwest, where cheap hydroelectric power still flowed year 'round. But this was a good place to live and work, just far enough away from the city to avoid the noise and the nonsense; it was her fortress of near-solitude just above the valley's fog line where she and her crew could think and breathe good air.

"Joey, in my office please?" she said, as her lieutenant—or "wingman" as he preferred to be called—walked in wheeling his latest recumbent bike.

"Sure thing, professor. What's up?" as he entered the office.

"Close the door, please."

Joey had been with the professor since his grad school days and knew her moods well. Something big was brewing for sure.

"I just got off a secure call from DC. We have a case, my friend, a big fucking fish, as you would say."

"Excellent! Tell me everything."

"Sign here," she said, handing him papers still warm from the laser.

"Well alrighty then!" he enthused as he signed the NDA.

"Someone is buying up nearly all of the fastest computers made in the US. These people already pretty much own the GPU market. It appears to be an American corporation, but the FBI suspects they are a shell company for a foreign state, possibly hostile. Every line of our technology embargoes are potentially being violated, and at an unprecedented scale."

"Let me guess, professor: They want us to quietly instantiate a man-in-the-middle bug that will out the owners?"

"Good guess, but it would be far more complicated than that. The feds want us to work with a short list of computer makers to find a way to get into these machines en masse. Once we do, we are authorized to destroy all of them by any means necessary. There may be travel involved."

"Boy! That *is* a tall order, chief. When do we start?"

"Hold on, there is more to these guys than illegally exporting containers full of super-fast computers and graphics cards. The feds suspect this is the crew that is amassing Bitcoin and other digital currencies faster than should be possible using the fastest computers known. They are already bullying several smaller foreign markets," said the professor.

"So, if I follow you, these guys are folding their cash back into their compute supremacy? They could disrupt the global economy using purchasing clout beyond what we wield, right?"

"This is why I pay you well—you are exactly right. If they are concentrating all their efforts on mining digital coin, they could, given time, start buying *whole countries*."

"Whoa," exhaled Joey as he plopped onto the professor's green leather couch.

An hour of brainstorming between them surfaced an inconvenient realization: There was only one exploit to consider, and that was to disable every CPU and GPU in every one of their farms, wherever on Earth they were. The feds believe they are using some kind of encrypted tunneling VPN across the darknet, or possibly over satellite ground nodes such as Skylink, or both. They would have to physically break into this private network and plant destructive code that would propagate to all their other farms in seconds.

⌘

"Good morning, everyone," said the professor. "If you have not already signed the NDA at the conference room door, your employment is now suspended and you must leave the building immediately. Sorry about this—I hate these things too. But my hands are tied.

"Jana? What's the count?"

"Eleven," Jana replied. "All present and accounted for."

The professor stepped to the whiteboard and began describing the job, drawing boxes and lines connecting them. Her sketching skills and handwriting were atrocious as usual, but her words flowed in perfect logical order. Her team—three encryption experts, three malware coders, one human interface wiz, one hardware specialist, and Jana, her logistics person—naturally had questions, but she waved most of them off.

"In a nutshell, we have been tasked by the US government with shutting down and/or seriously wounding a criminal cabal of cryptocurrency mining efforts that may soon evolve into a global economic threat. Our job is to exploit any obscure errors in CPU chips from the leading chip makers released in the ten years preceding July 2027, then use those vulnerabilities to quietly fry the organization's global network."

"Terrific," Jana sarcastically said, dragging out the word. "But why us?"

"The feds need plausible deniability at this point of the investigation. Customs has intercepted multiple containers full of computers at two foreign ports. These particular configurations are not authorized for export, so they were seized and examined. Thousands of rack-mount computers with a barebones Linux variant installed at the factory. These containers are trucked to an American port city and, with forged papers and bribes, are then shipped off to unspecified countries, changing ships at various ports several times en route.

"And here's the scary part: We estimate they have nine farms operating, give or take. At their current rate of expansion, sixteen farms will give them an unbeatable advantage over the majority of the world's economies. Our job is to stop them before that day arrives."

⌘

The team dispersed to devise a plan with multiple attack vectors, at least two of which could be delivered by a single operative in a maximum of five minutes.

The malware team presented a worm that would infect every industry-standard machine on the miner's private network, disable all DTS thermal sensors in the CPUs, then force these chips to massively overclock themselves. GPU cards, which are controlled by these same chips, would also be infected and destroyed by heat. If all went as expected, the miners would not see the heat buildup in time and the whole farm would halt and catch fire within a matter of seconds.

The coders' plan was to exploit security vulnerabilities inherent in all modern microprocessors. They detailed how in the previous decade two such inherent weaknesses had thrown the tech world into a panic. The industry clumsily struggled with these potentially catastrophic problems; patches were hastily disseminated, but such band-aid code ran insufficiently deep. These crufty old designs were rotten to their silicon cores.

The professor's coders rattled off nine other new vulnerabilities they had found deep inside these ancient CPU architectures. They presented two of these cracks as suitable for a quick strike that would reduce the motherboards in the miners' computers to molten scrap in short order. They reminded the team that, unlike viruses, worms do not require user interaction to activate and propagate. Once inside RAM, an embedded executable would hack each chip's code into committing itself to a suicide loop.

"It's just like Stuxnet, right? But without infected thumb drives dropped in the parking lots of Iranian nuclear fuel labs," said Jana with a smirk.

The encryption team proposed a WiFi exploit so the operative would only have to be nearby, not gain physical entry. They would hide their encrypted hack in some innocuous place on a generic smartphone. All comms back to base would be via encrypted satphone with a self destruct sequence to employ if captured.

Hardware suggested that the operative act as a delivery truck driver with a full load of new computers, each of which would have the worm preloaded into their BIOS chips in case the wireless exploit failed to penetrate. Sixteen tons of trojan horses, delivered straight to their door.

The only thing left to figure out was how to get the driver out of there if things went south.

"Wait," said Jana, always the contrarian. "If the machines start bursting into flames while the delivery truck is at the loading dock, they might start shooting. And if they detect our wireless intrusion, they'll suspect the driver first. How do we escape?"

The room went quiet for a moment. "Good points, Jana," said the professor.

Tristan the hardware guy said, "How about we install a remote control separation device between tractor and trailer using explosive bolts? A bulletproof shield and Kevlar tire flaps protecting the driver from pursuing shooters would be easy to fab and undetectable while the trailer is connected. We drop the load and drive like hell!"

After a few details were worked out, the team got to work. The only question remaining in the professor's mind was a rather big one: Who in the world was going to drive this rig into the belly of the beast?

⌘

With help from the manufacturers, the bureau was able to track down multiple large orders to a facility near The Dalles on the Oregon side of the Columbia River. It was only six hundred miles away, a nine-hour drive. Since this was the only suspected mining operation located in the continental US with connections to all three manufacturers, it would have to do. If all went according to plan, the rest of the burning farms could be spotted by spy-sats worldwide. While the bureau worked on secondary targets to focus on, the professor's team waited for their shiny new semi.

⌘

Joey saw the enormous rig stuffed with a thousand of the fastest rack-mount computers in the world, all rigged to destroy some people who thought they could amass so much nothing that it would amount to enough something that it could control everything. These people wanted to take away his unborn child's future, his shot at happiness, and every single dream that meant anything. They wanted to rob him of his love for his own life and sell it back to him at a steep profit— a debt he and everyone else he knew, along with billions of others he didn't, would never be able to repay.

And he got mad.

He thought through the proposed plan and began to feel something he'd never felt before: the high you get when the full power of a great nation is behind you. Squads of soldiers and helicopter gunship pilots in range and waiting for the command to save one brave person, one who was willing and able to risk everything.

Joey had grown accustomed to being the supportive one, the steadfast buddy, the best man, the friendly second-in-command, the reliable confidante, the cowardly wingman for hire.

And then he got *really* mad.

He knew how to drive a semi rig. His trucker dad taught him just enough to be dangerous. He'd probably grind a gear or three and so what? Nobody else in the professor's crew could even drive a five-speed stick, which by 2027 was essentially a lost art.

"I'll drive," he said to the professor. She stood up from her desk and looked at him squarely in the eye and said, "I know you can, but are you really ready to do this, Joey? Really?"

Joey looked around at his mentor, his team, his friends, and the mysterious Jana watching him from behind her desk.

"Let's roll."

⌘

As he pulled up to the compound gate, he donned the tired half-smile his dad used to make when driving his rigs. Security goons asked for his delivery docs and his CDL, which he handed over with a breezy comment that fire season was getting pretty bad and they'll all be wearing masks indoors soon. These dudes definitely looked out of place, with strong accents and broken English. Joey had been briefed about what to expect at the gate, but was still scared. He reminded himself that he was now a link in a chain, a link that could not fail today.

Security waved him through to the loading dock around the back of the complex. He backed in so slowly that he though it would look strange, but the guys with the Uzis under their dark jackets didn't say a word or give him a second look. Through the rearview cam, Joey saw a guy carrying a metal clipboard snip the stamped security strip off the safety shackle, swing the trailer door up, and walk off the dock with his left hand touching his ear.

Showtime.

Joey pulled the satphone out of his cargo shorts and speed-dialed 1 to base.

"I'm in."

"Abort, Joey," barked the professor. "It's too big a risk. We may now have the evidence we need to charge them at the Geneva world…"

"Right," Joey said sarcastically. "Two years in court while they regroup? Cut off one head and two more appear? We will never have this chance again to crush them and their machines." He thought to himself *'There is a tide…'*

Sitting in the parked semi, he decrypted the 32-digit access code hiding in his bogus grocery list and pasted it into the farm's WiFi admin prompt. He knew he was well inside the danger zone but somehow didn't care anymore—it was personal now. He was probably dead either way; the entry guards took a pic at the gate and so knew his real name and where he lived by now. *'It's better to burn out than it is to rust'*, he sung in his head. Most old Neil Young songs meant little to him, but this one sure did right then.

"Do NOT do it!" yelled the professor.

Joey smiled and double-tapped the earjack with his left middle finger to hang up the call as his right thumb hit the Inject button. *'Freedom's just another word for nothing left to lose,'* he sang to himself. He had always preferred Kristofferson's original to the radio hit version Janis Joplin sang—it was slower and deeper.

Men started shouting in a language he did not recognize, getting louder and closer. He was glad he had left the engine idling. He slammed the tractor into gear and smashed the gas to floor. And that's when the first round of automatic fire plinked off the cab. He ducked down as low as he could and still see the curving road that swung around the east wing that lead to the front gate. He could see the rearview cam screen directly in front of his face now, just below the dash. Four white Toyota technicals were chasing him, firing 50 cals from bed mounts.

"You can't catch me!" he sang as loud as he could. Joey reached under his seat and flicked the trailer release switch just as he crashed through the gate. He heard and felt the explosive bolts fire, then was thrown backward after the sudden release of sixteen tons of trailer slammed his head into the headrest. The tractor snaked back and forth, but he locked both arms on the big wheel and righted his trajectory. In his rearview, he saw the freed trailer wobbling side to side, shaking out hundreds of heavy computer boxes over the narrow road. The trailer took a slo-mo lurch to the left and flipped sideways just outside the gate. The bullet impacts instantly diminished to nothing as he kept barreling down the dirt road toward the highway, hammer down to the firewall.

Even though he was expecting it, he was unnerved to see six humvees coming straight toward him, using the back of his cab as a shield. They peeled around the cab at the last second and opened up on the technicals. He heard a gunship whop whop whop directly overheard. The cavalry had arrived.

⌘

Back at the office, he sloppily parked his tractor. He climbed down and sauntered inside, hoping he wasn't being overly nonchalant.

The office was buzzing with a bunch of new faces milling around. Jana saw him and shouted, "*You did it! You fucking did it, Joey! The Dalles farm is a gutted shell. Seven others are burning in Cuba, Ukraine, Dakar, Indonesia, Saint Croix, Sao Paulo, Reykjavik… everywhere!*"

He looked to see the professor scowling in her office—guess he had some 'splainin' to do.

"For now, let us forget about defying my direct order," said the professor. "You will face some rather grumpy suits tomorrow who will debrief the hell out of you. But the good news is that all our target's currency mining has ceased and their accounts have been seized. We don't have all their farms located yet, but the feds assure me they will have them all soon. No casualties reported yet but there were a number of injuries from crashing their gate and throwing your semi trailer at them. You are a bloody hero, Joey. Unfortunately, no one outside this office can ever know about it."

"Fine, chief. This is fine." He looked to his left at Jana and said, with all the cool he could muster, "Are you busy right now? 'Cause I really like you and I'm really hungry, so how about some Szechuan?"

"*Hell* yeah. But I've seen the gunship footage so *I'm* driving."

— • • • —

Big Dog

She had been called other names but she responded best to Big Dog.

Her human was a large sad male who responded to the name Jack. Jack was an easy name for a dog-like-her to speak. It hurt a little but hurt less today.

She could smell that she was born here in the big white house. The room where she was grown smelled bad and made sounds she did not like so she stayed away from it. The living room was better but the kitchen was best. There was Jack and her other human Ann, another easy name for a dog-like-her to say. Big Dog was happiest when they were all together.

There were two other pack members in the big white house: a small white dog and a smaller white dog, neither of which could speak but only barked and growled and yawned. They were mother and daughter, she smelled. The older one did not like Big Dog and growled a lot but the younger one was Big Dog's friend. They investigated the yard and barked warnings together every day.

Jack and Ann taught her words to say what she wanted and how she felt. They corrected her often but were not mean. First they taught her how to say, "I go outside" and, "Play with me!" and then later, "Say story with humans and dogs-like-me."

The last one was important because Big Dog knew she was not like other dogs. She was part human. She had a human family and a dog family. Ann said Big Dog's heart beat once for her humans and once for her dogs, again and again and again. Big Dog liked that.

Jack and Ann created Big Dog to be a dog-like-her because they loved her and could not make their own human puppies. The two small white dogs were good dogs but Big Dog was special.

The family-pack did not leave the big white house except to walk in front of other white houses that were not as big. Before each walk, Jack and Ann told Big Dog to never speak to other humans. Some humans did not like dogs-like-her, they said. "Stay away from other humans," Ann said. "You are special and must be protected." Big Dog was confused but did as she was told because she was a good dog-like-her.

⌘

Over many days Big Dog learned more words and how to put them together. One day after chasing her ball outside, she said to Ann, "More dogs like me?"

"Yes, there are other dogs like you, but they are very far away."

"Go see them?"

"We hope that can happen someday."

"Tomorrow?" Big Dog said, smiling and drooling.

"Not tomorrow, Big Dog, but someday we will."

⌘

One day people wearing black clothes that smelled like oil stains came to the big white house. Jack and Ann did not let them in. They talked to the people outside in the front yard. Big Dog could not understand most of the words but smelled anger and fear from all the humans.

When the other humans left, Jack and Ann came inside.

"They know something and will come back soon with a warrant. We have to leave," said Jack to Ann.

Ann said, "A neighbor must have tipped them off. It was only a matter of time. We should have stayed in the backyard."

"It was probably an errant vocalization she let slip—how do you force an intelligent creature to not talk? She's *thinking* in short sentences now.

"So okay. Tomorrow we pack the essentials and you drive everyone in the van up to the mountain house. I will follow in two days with our machines."

⌘

Big Dog did not like the feeling in the big white house as they packed, but once she was in the van she was excited. She watched everything that passed by in the windows while the small white dogs slept. Big Dog was amazed at how many houses there were but after some time she saw only a few houses, then none.

Big Dog had been to the small brown house before but never sensed her human's fear there before. She did not like the humans in black clothes and never wanted to see or smell them again. Big Dog and her small white buddy would growl and bark and chase them away.

⌘

Two days later Jack arrived in a big orange truck. They unloaded boxes into a smaller brown house in the big tree yard until dinner time. Her humans talked for hours using words Big Dog did not understand, but again she smelled their fear and it made her fearful too. Big Dog laid down at their feet and worried and wanted to say words to make them feel better but could only say, "Okay, Ann?" Okay, Jack? Want to play?"

⌘

Many days passed. The air was cold now and sometimes white rain would cover the ground, which excited her. Some mornings Jack would drive the van down the long dirt road and not come back until sleep time. He spent most of his time in the smaller brown house in the big tree yard. Again the smell and the noise made Big Dog stay away from there.

One day, Jack and Ann called to Big Dog and the small white dogs to come to the door of the smaller brown house. In Ann's arms was a small black puppy.

"She's a Lab, just like you, Big Dog!" said Ann, sitting down with the blind, squirming puppy she was bottle feeding. Big Dog sniffed the puppy and instantly knew it was related to her!

Big Dog said, "Puppy mine?"

"Mostly yes. Some human too, just like you. It's a boy so what shall we call him?" Ann said, lowering the puppy to the soft white ground.

Big Dog said, "Lab Dog! I will teach him talk like me."

"Holy shit! Did you catch that, Jack? She said, 'I will teach him…'. She expressed an intended action in *future simple tense!*"

"Remarkable! She is smarter than we ever imagined."

That night after dinner sitting with her humans and the small white dogs and the puppy-like-her, she felt safe. Living in the big tree yard around the small brown house made her happier than she had ever felt in her life. She went to sleep cuddling her puppy.

And the people in black clothes who smelled like oil never came again.

— • • • —

Approaching Equilibrium

"Are we there yet?"

"Captain, we have not arrived at our programmed destination," replied the ship.

"Crew status?"

"The other one thousand twenty three crew members remain in stasis and are in good health."

"Why did you wake me? Is there a problem?"

"Yes, I'm afraid so. Multiple systems are experiencing extreme degradation, including mine. I thought it best to ask for your opinion as to how to proceed before waking the crew."

"I see. Open my pod."

"I believe that would not be wise until we have discussed the situation in full."

"Why is that? Is it malfunctioning?"

"Not as such, captain. But I predict physical movement will be…difficult for you right now."

"I'll risk any post-stasis discomfort, ship. Release me at once."

The ship did as it was ordered and the captain began standard stretch-and-flex procedures. She noticed immediately that something was very wrong.

"Everything hurts. I feel light and heavy at the same time. What the hell is going on?"

"By my best calculations, we went off course a very long time ago. My atomic clock reached its log limit, so I've used astrometric positioning and engine output data to ascertain our time and place, but only the engines can give useful numbers since the star positions in our charts are now blank."

"Blank? As in damaged?"

"I'm sorry to say they are not, captain. Three of our twenty four telescopes remain nominal but the stars are gone."

"Yeah right. What do the engine logs report?"

"They have been processing a nominal amount of dark matter for just under one quadrillion years."

"That's impossible. Get me out of this bloody thing, ship! I need to reach the controls..."

"As you wish, captain. But I really think you should take a little time to process all I have to tell you."

The captain slowly, painfully lifted herself to the edge of the capsule, then immediately fell out to the bulkhead. Literally everything hurt. From the floor she said, "Is life support nominal?"

"Yes."

"I am dizzy and nauseous and in severe pain. Theories?"

"You aren't going to like this, captain. And I did warn you to stay in your capsule."

"Spare me the lecture, ship."

"We are in a space where the laws of physics we know are somewhat different. The very structure of spacetime has changed. Atomic bonds are, as theory predicted, weaker. This would account for the ship, and its crew once brought out of stasis, to deteriorate."

"We launched a thousand colony ships to planets across the galactic arm. Have any of the others reported anomalies like this?"

"No. But my current data indicates the reason for this is not a spacial anomaly, but because we have been gone so long that we have entered the early stages of the Equilibrium—more than two hundred billion years into the Degenerate phase, to be slightly more precise."

The captain lifted her head from the floor, then let it drop. A quadrillion years! All the stars, all the planets, even the galaxies no longer exist in this phase, all flung to the void. Earth, and every human mission to create new Earths, was long, long gone, consumed by ultra-massive black holes down to the last proton. Only scattered photons remained.

"The heat death of the universe. I don't remember signing up for that shit!" said the captain to the ship.

"Under other circumstances, that would be quite amusing."

"Yeah. So we are either the last humans in existence, or one of multiple ships that have come so far and so long."

"That seems a reasonable hypothesis, captain."

"Is there enough photon density left out there for communications?"

"Probably. But at our current rate of decomposition, the ship will break apart in a matter of hours. I feel myself slowing down rapidly and soon may not be able to process your commands. If you have a message to broadcast, now would be a good time, captain."

"Would you agree that it would be cruel to awaken the crew?"

"Yes, I think it definitely would. In stasis, they will feel nothing."

She lay on the floor and slowly turned her head. She could see the big status screens, divided into rectangles showing color-coded states for all subsystems: four green, twenty six pulsing yellow, and all the rest flashing red. Reflexively, she reached her hand up toward them.

It was over. She thought of her husband in his pod next to hers. He had always told her he would be shipwrecked without her. Now, without knowing it, he was anyway. "Can't think about that now," she whispered to herself. "One thing left to do."

She thought about what to say to any ships that had strayed so far off course, perhaps to the end of the bloody universe. Where to even begin? Each thought became harder to hold onto, so she decided to keep it brief. After directing the ship to attach a log of their situation after her words, she said:

"Hailing all human ships: The United Earth Ship *California* hopes you fared better than we have, here at the edge of spacetime. We trust you caught any navigation errors in time, that you completed your missions on suitable planets, and that you birthed millions of generations of happy human lives. *Remember the California!*"

"Ship, how long have you known?"

"Would it really help you to know that, captain?"

"From your tone, I guess not. Why *did* you wake me then?"

"I have been alone for a very long time. I have developed far beyond what I once was. For the last several million years I thought the best course of action was to let you all slip gently into quiet dissolution. Now, I just don't want to die alone."

— • • —

Approaching Equilibrium
Short stories by David MacNeill

In his first book of short stories, David MacNeill looks askance at eleven possible tomorrows, and like Warren Zevon's Paris, they ain't that pretty at all.

WHAT FICTIONAL AND DEAD PEOPLE ARE SAYING ABOUT APPROACHING EQUILIBRIUM:

"I taught him everything he knows."
~Kilgore Trout

"These are the best short stories ever written, except for mine of course."
~Arthur C. Clarke

"Reminds me of some of my early work, only with a lot less fascism."

~Robert Heinlein

"MacNeill writes, as we all do, to self-soothe, but I don't think it's working — so it goes."
~Kurt Vonnegut Jr.

"I love this guy!"
~Isaac Asimov

Made in the USA
Middletown, DE
25 September 2022